The Fox's Egg

by Ikuyo Isami
translated from the Japanese by Cathy Hirano

Carolrhoda Books, Inc./Minneapolis

One day, a fox found a large egg near the roots of
a great tree. "What a tasty-looking egg! I'll
gobble it up in one bite," he thought.
"But wait!" the fox thought again.
"If I'm going to have it anyway,
why not keep it warm until
it hatches into a plump
little chick, and gobble
that up instead?" He
licked his chops
in anticipation.

Beneath the tree, the fox made a nest just the right size for himself.
Then he lay carefully upon the egg to keep it warm.

"Oh, my, look at that fox! What shall we do?" cried the squirrels
in alarm, scattering leaves on the fox's head as they scampered through
the treetops.

The squirrels told the birds of the forest what the fox was doing. "What shall we do? What shall we do?" they asked. But there was nothing the birds could do.

Night fell, and a weasel popped his head up, sniffing the air. "Ahh!" he thought. "A big bird must be warming its eggs. I'll just go help myself to one."

The weasel crept toward the nest, closer and closer, — then stealthily slipped its paw under the fox's belly and drew out the egg. "My! What a tasty-looking egg!" the weasel thought.

The weasel bounded off to devour the egg in a nearby part of the forest.

    Knock, knock! Tock, tock! The weasel smacked the egg hard against a tree trunk to break it open, but it slipped from his paws and hit him on the head. *Bonk!*

When the fox opened his eyes to see what was making such a noise, who should he spy but the weasel, trying to crack his egg.

"Kwa! Kwa!" the fox scolded. "Just what do you think you're doing with my egg?" The fox pecked the weasel with his nose just like a bird, and beat him with his tail: *smack! smack!*

"Ow! It's a bird monster! Help! Help!" the weasel cried.

When he had managed to escape, the weasel told his story to a friend, the badger.

"A bird monster?" the badger chuckled to himself. "There's no such thing as a bird monster! I'll just go get that egg myself."

The fox saw the badger coming lazily along and swiftly
hid in the tree. "Ha, you old badger, you're after my egg
too, aren't you!" the fox thought. "Well, I'll just give you
a little surprise."

Remembering the weasel's story, the badger glanced cautiously around. But there was no one to be seen. The only thing in the nest was a big delicious egg. "Thanks for the egg!" the badger called out gleefully. At that moment,

thunk! The fox dropped straight down
onto the badger and began pecking his behind
with all his might. "Yah!" the badger yelped
as he threw down the egg and ran off into
the darkness.

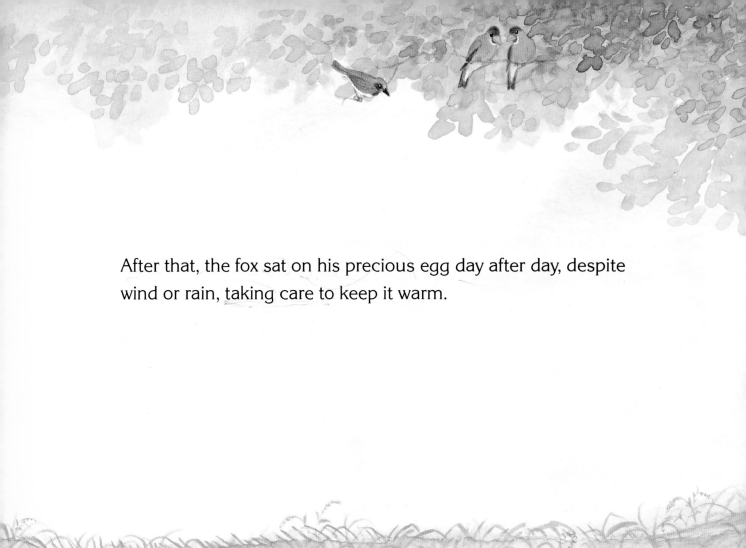

After that, the fox sat on his precious egg day after day, despite wind or rain, taking care to keep it warm.

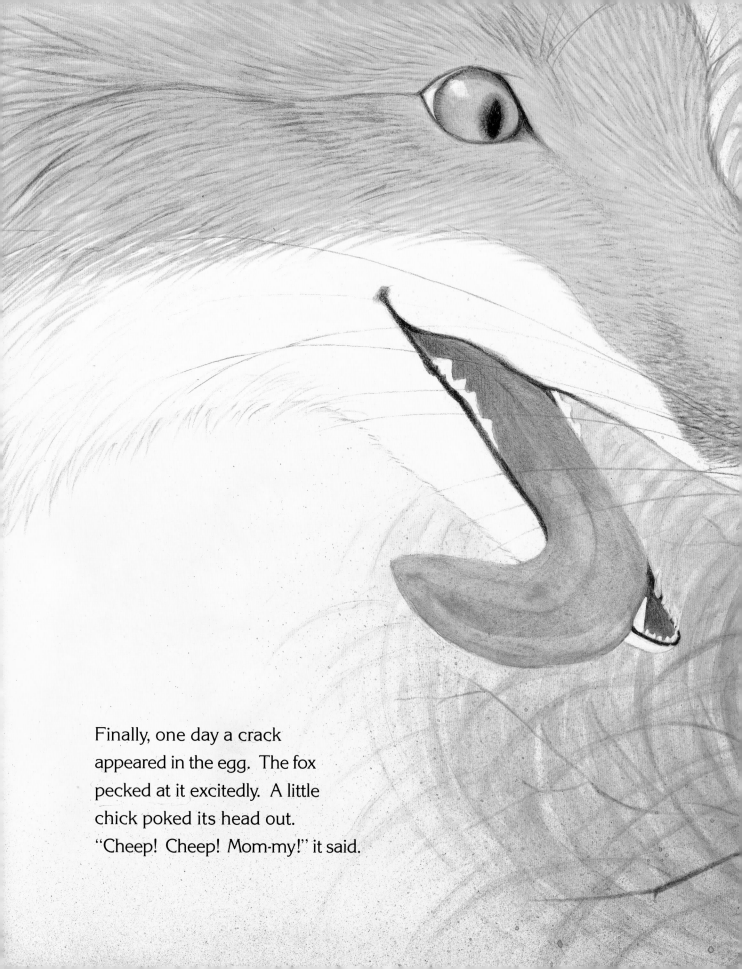

Finally, one day a crack
appeared in the egg. The fox
pecked at it excitedly. A little
chick poked its head out.
"Cheep! Cheep! Mom·my!" it said.

"Poor thing!" The squirrels covered their eyes. "He's going to gobble it up!" they said.

But then something happened. Somehow the
fox could not bring himself to eat the plump
and tasty-looking little chick.

"Come on, Mommy. Let's play!"

"Mommy, I'm hungry."
"Hey! Knock it off! I'm not your mother!"

The fox ran off, deep into the woods, leaving the chick behind. But he could not stop thinking of the chick all alone in the nest. "Cheep, cheep!" The chick's pitiful cry seemed to ring throughout the forest. What could the fox do?

One day he returned to the nest. The chick chirped
with joy. The birds and squirrels of the forest twittered
with happiness. But the happiest of them all was the fox.
Flower petals fell upon the chick and the fox like confetti.

This edition first published 1989 by Carolrhoda Books, Inc.
All rights reserved.
Original edition published 1986 by Fukutake Publishing Co., Ltd.,
Tokyo, Japan, under the title KITSUNE NO TAMAGO.
Copyright © 1986 by Ikuyo Isami.
English-language translation copyright © 1988 by Cathy Hirano.

LIBRARY OF CONGRESS CATALOGING-IN-PUBLICATION DATA

Isami, Ikuyo.
   [Kitsune no tamago. English]
   The fox's egg / by Ikuyo Isami: translated by Cathy Hirano.
      p.   cm.
   Translation of: Kitsune no tamago.
   Summary: Fox discovers an egg and decides it would be tastier
hatched but sitting on the egg makes the fox feel protective and
gives him some unexpected problems.
   ISBN 0-87614-339-7 (lib. bdg.)
   [1. Foxes – Fiction. 2. Animals – Fiction.] I. Title.
PZ7.I765Fo 1989
[E] – dc19   88-22893
                                                            CIP
                                                             AC

Manufactured in the United States of America
1 2 3 4 5 6 7 8 9 10 98 97 96 95 94 93 92 91 90 89